Praise for Storyshares

"One of the brightest innovators and game-changers in the education industry."
— Forbes

"Your success in applying research-validated practices to promote literacy serves as a valuable model for other organizations seeking to create evidence-based literacy programs." — Library of Congress

"We need powerful social and educational innovation, and Storyshares is breaking new ground. The organization addresses critical problems facing our students and teachers. I am excited about the strategies it brings to the collective work of making sure every student has an equal chance in life."
— Teach For America

"It's the perfect idea. There's really nothing like this. I mean, wow, this will be a wonderful experience for young people." — Andrea Davis Pinkney, Executive Director, Scholastic

"Reading for meaning opens opportunities for a lifetime of learning. Providing emerging readers with engaging texts that are designed to offer both challenges and support for each individual will improve their lives for years to come. Storyshares is a wonderful start."
— David Rose, Co-founder of CAST & UDL

An Indian Summer

Storyshares presents

Published by Storyshares, LLC
Inspiring reading with a new kind of book.

The characters and events in this book are fictitious. Any similarity
to real persons, living or dead, is entirely coincidental.

Storyshares
Storyshares, LLC
24 N. Bryn Mawr Avenue #340
Bryn Mawr, Pennsylvania 19010-3304
www.storyshares.org

Interest Level: High School
Grade Level Equivalent: 5.6

ISBN 9798885977234
Book design by Saskia Globig

AN INDIAN SUMMER

Pravallika Kullampalle

Storyshares

CONTENTS

CHAPTER ONE

He carefully surveyed my face before taking hold of my cheek, squeezing it tight enough to turn my cinnamon complexion rosy.

"Ow!" I cried out as I rubbed my cheek.

Would I ever grow out of this greeting? I wondered as I looked up at a man who beamed down at me.

"Look at how much you have grown, Anni! You look just like *Nana*. You know, they say it is good fortune when a daughter looks like her father," my *babai* said as he handed me a bouquet of roses that had given into the heat of the monsoon season. "Now, tell me, how was your journey? I was worried when you told me you were flying alone."

He took the handle of the cart of suitcases in front of me.

"The journey was good, *Babai*, my ears didn't pop when we were landing, thank God. See, I told you that you were worried for nothing," I answered in Telugu, hoping my false confidence would mask the panic attack I had moments earlier.

My thoughts had run to worst-case scenarios as I struggled to balance a backpack, a camera slung over my shoulder, and a cart of suitcases. The airport terminal was filled with cab drivers holding signs with the names of people I didn't know and anxious family members holding "welcome home" signs.

As my eyes drifted from eager faces to impatient ones, a bubble of panic started to rise within me. It wasn't until I set my eyes on a dark, broad-shouldered man in a worn checkered flannel who waved his hands high above his head that I stopped and took a deep breath. The bubble burst inside me as I pushed my cart in my uncle's direction.

CHAPTER TWO

"Welcome to India!" he had exclaimed, just like the last time I saw him, and the time before.

Our conversation went on as my *babai* pushed the cart up through the airport's parking lot. A tall, balding man, dressed similarly to my *babai*, waved his hand as we approached him.

"The luggage, I will put, you sit in car. You have good journey?" the driver asked in broken English as he pointed toward the car.

I stifled a giggle before answering. "Driver Uncle, *Nenu Telugu Matladuthaanu. Journey baaga ayindi.*"

I speak Telugu. *Yes, the journey went well.*

After close to twenty-four hours of traveling, it felt good to breathe in the outdoor air around me. The humid air smelled of the airport's outdoor food court and a sleeping city. I settled into the window seat of the car as the driver and my *babai* worked to tie the suitcases to the top of the car.

I rolled down the windows and closed my eyes. My favorite part of the journey still lay ahead of me: a four-hour drive from the Bangalore Airport to the small town of Pantapalli. After the driver and my babai settled into their seats, we were off.

CHAPTER THREE

"You must be hungry, Anni. *Pinni* has made some snacks for you. *Amma* told me that you love *pabbillalu* and *murukulu*," my *babai* said. He offered me an opened tin container of deep-fried rice flour chips.

"Thanks, *Babai!*" I said as I munched on the flavor-packed rice chips. "Oh, these are so good! *Amma* also makes these back home. Driver Uncle, please, take some snacks. You also must be tired. It is four in the morning!" I handed the container to the driver. "I can promise you that you have never tasted *murukulu* like these!"

He chuckled before taking one himself. "You're right, even my wife does not make snacks like this. Don't tell her I said that," he said as he crunched on the snacks and winked at me in the mirror.

I smiled back at him before turning my attention back to my uncle.

"Tell me, *Babai*, what's new?" I asked.

"Well, not much has changed since you spoke to us before you got on the plane. How are *Amma*, *Nana*, and your brother Saish doing?" he asked.

"They're all fine, nothing new there. I honestly cannot tell you how excited I am to be able to see everyone after three years," I said. "The last time I was here, I was fifteen. So much has happened, and even though I call and talk to all of you, I feel like I have missed so much."

"And that's why you're here! You have an entire trip ahead of you to make up for all you have missed. Don't think you are the only one who feels that way; we missed seeing you grow up, too. Just look at you, all grown up. We couldn't be prouder of the young woman you are today," he said, holding up my chin. "That's why everyone is excited when any of you come home." He gave me a soft smile.

CHAPTER FOUR

After a moment of silence, he turned to me again. "I am going to close my eyes for a bit. Don't hesitate to wake me up if you need anything. You should also sleep. I don't know how much you slept on the plane ride here. I know that the car isn't very comfortable, but try and get some rest, at least. Everyone is eagerly waiting for you at home, and they won't let you rest once we reach it," he said as I smiled. "We'll stop and get breakfast in an hour or two."

He pressed his head against the tattered seat and dozed off. I closed my eyes and rested my head against the window as I breathed in the air that flooded into the car.

I looked out the window, thinking of all the cousins who grew up before I had a chance to hold them, the grandparents I had only met once or twice, and the memories I hadn't had the chance to make with my family.

You're here now; make the most of it, I reminded myself as I opened my eyes and watched the streets pass by.

CHAPTER FIVE

There was a certain moment when the city's atmosphere faded away and was replaced by the incense of earthy roads and a sense of calm not found in the city.

It was around six in the morning now, and the villages and towns we passed through slowly came to life. Mothers in nightgowns ran back and forth. They were trying to pack lunches for their husbands and children while they tackled the tangled messes of their daughters' long hair, trying to tie it up into braids for school. The fresh morning was filled with chatter as some watched our car pass by.

I found it interesting that even though my parents immigrated to America twenty-three years ago, my mornings had been filled with the same busyness I watched through the window.

My mom, who I called *Amma*, always woke up before the rest of us. She took a shower and completed her *pooja* before dragging my brother and me out of bed. As my brother and I got ready for school, she would make a steaming hot cup of coffee for my dad, prepare a hearty breakfast, and pack lunches for all of us while we ran around trying to find everything for the day. After we left for school and my dad went to work, she would make herself a cup of coffee and sit in her favorite chair near the window that overlooked our garden.

I smiled to myself as I waved to the children who reminded me of my younger self.

CHAPTER SIX

As we passed by the villages, one woman who stood in a brightly colored *saree* caught my eye. She reached for a broom and swept the dust that had gathered overnight in front of her doorstep. She scooped her hands into a copper vessel and splattered water all over the surface, and then began.

Bending down, she scooped white flour into her hand and slowly released small amounts to form a pattern of dots. She then looped the dots into families by drawing lines between them. As she stepped away, a larger pattern emerged; she began to smile.

It wasn't the first time I had seen someone draw this pattern of dots and lines. My mom would create similar designs with a piece of chalk whenever we celebrated festivals such as Diwali. *Amma* had explained to me that the ritual of drawing a *muggu* in front of a home every morning was a symbol of family.

"No matter how far one dot is from another, it will always be looped into the pattern. Remember, no matter how far you go, those lines of relationships you build will always tie you to this family," she had said to me.

On trips to India, my own *muggu* would expand with every new relative I met. The lines connecting me to known relatives were strengthened. However, just as a *muggu* fades, so did my relationships with my family.

On leaving day, I would wipe away my tears, making empty promises to keep in touch and call every week. Each empty promise worked as an eraser on the lines I had built with my family.

I felt tears well up in my eyes before I caught the driver's glance in the mirror and smiled back.

CHAPTER SEVEN

"Everything ok? You look deep in thought," he said.

"Ya, Uncle, I'm just tired from my journey," I said, trying to keep a steady voice as he smiled a little.

"My younger daughter is in sixth grade. She wants to grow up and go somewhere foreign, like you!" he said in Telugu. "Maybe in a couple of years, I will be picking her up from the airport, taking her home."

I watched pride gleam in his eyes. I smiled and nodded, not knowing how to answer.

"I'm kind of hungry, can we stop some-where for breakfast?" I asked.

"There is a *dosa* place nearby; we can stop there. Wake your *babai*; he must be hungry, too. We started from home at midnight and he was so eager to see you at the airport, he didn't sleep a wink," he said as he looked at my *babai* through the mirror.

At the *dhaba*, the waiter brought me a hot plate of *dosa* with a side of sambar and chut-ney. We were all hungry and ate in silence.

Although the *dosas* were not crispy enough, the sambar was too liquidy, and the chutney was too salty, I said nothing as I stuffed my mouth with something that could cure my hunger.

My mom's cooking, on the other hand, was perfect and was popular among my friends and guests. Every time someone sat down for a meal at my place, they always left with a full belly and never-ending praise for my mom's food.

CHAPTER EIGHT

"Do you like the *dosa*?" my *babai* asked.

"It's all right. But, never would I eat it like that!" I exclaimed as I pointed to the atrocity my *babai* was committing.

He tore a piece off the dosa and dipped it into the sambar and then into the chutney before placing it in his mouth. In my eyes, this was like eating fries dipped in a mix of ranch and ketchup.

"Oh come on, this is the real secret to enjoying *dosa* properly!" he said, grinning as I shook my head.

"No, that's disgusting," I said, as we shared a chuckle.

"Do you want a cup of coffee?" *Babai* asked me.

"I don't drink coffee," I said.

The only exception to this was my mom's coffee. Every once in a while, she would make a special kind of filter coffee that tasted better than any drink Starbucks could ever brew up. Gosh, how much I missed her and her cooking.

I had just completed my third year in college, and instead of going back home after finals, I decided to fly straight to India. I found tickets in the first week of June and quickly booked them. Before I knew it, I was sitting in an airplane, ready to fly halfway across the world on my own. I was so glad that in a couple of weeks, my mom, dad, and brother would also be coming to India.

CHAPTER NINE

It wasn't long before we drove into the village that looked like the one I remembered visiting when I was younger.

Although Pantapalli had changed since the last time I was there, the village's spirit remained evergreen. The increase in rainfall in recent years had led to a successful crop year. Palm trees waved in the warm breeze of the mid-morning and bright green rice paddies decorated small reservoirs of water. Nature seemed to welcome the monsoon season with a festivity of its own.

Many of the small houses had been replaced by larger, two-story, concrete buildings that were painted vibrantly. Men in worn white shirts, *lungis*—a cotton cloth wrapped around the waist that extended to the ankle—and a towel wrapped around their heads walked on the side of the road. They were herding their cows to their fields. The cows here did not moo like they did back home. Instead, they bellowed a long *ambaa* as we drove past them.

After a long journey, we finally arrived. The colorfully painted concrete house sat in the middle of our small farmland. To the right of the house was a small shed where the cows were housed.

CHAPTER TEN

As soon as the car drove up to the house, cousins came running out of the gates. They threw open the SUV doors and tackled me into a hug.

"We missed you so much! Welcome to India!" they said as they squeezed me tight.

"I missed you all, too!" I said as I threw my arms around them.

Six years, I thought to myself. *How did six years go by since the last time I was here?*

I had promised myself to never forget the memories, to never forget the relationships

I'd spent a summer building. How many of those promises had I kept?

I stepped onto the concrete platform that surrounded the house. I looked up to see an eager crowd, their warm smiles radiating down the walkway. As I walked toward the house, Lilly, my aunt's dog, welcomed me with a loud "Woof Woof!" My aunt struggled to not fall over as Lilly rushed toward me and dragged my aunt with her.

"Lilly! How are you? I know, I know, I missed you, too!" I said as she jumped up and gave me a wet kiss.

I stood up and saw my grandparents, my *attas*, *mamas*, *annas*, *akkas*, *pinnis*, *babai*, and so many other family members standing in front of me, grinning. The ground had been decorated with a beautiful *muggu* that spelled out "Welcome Home Anamika!"

The *muggu* had been drawn largely with flowers decorating the dots and lines.

This time, no empty promises. I am the artist of my muggu. *I will learn to redraw these lines and make them permanent*, I thought to myself.

CHAPTER ELEVEN

I looked up to see my cousin approaching me with a plate in her hand. It was custom that anytime someone arrived from a long journey, they were to be welcomed into the home after an *Aarati*. It was a ritual where a camphor piece was set on fire and circled in front of someone, to get rid of *Dhishti*, the evil eye.

After the *Aarati* had finished, I approached my grandparents and bowed in front of them. I touched my fingers to their feet before moving my hands towards my eyes as they blessed me. A round of hugs was exchanged, and suitcases were unloaded from the car with the help of everyone around me.

After taking a deep breath, I finally took a step inside the house that I would learn to call home. This was the beginning of my Indian summer.

About the Author

Pravallika Kullampalle is a contributing author to the Storyshares library.

About the Publisher

Storyshares is a publisher focused on supporting the millions of teens and adults who struggle with reading by creating a new shelf in the library specifically for them. The ever-growing collection features content that is compelling and culturally relevant for teens and adults, yet still readable at a range of lower reading levels.

Storyshares generates content by engaging deeply with writers, bringing together a community to create this new kind of book. With more intriguing and approachable stories to choose from, the teens and adults who have fallen behind are improving their skills and beginning to discover the joy of reading.
For more information, visit storyshares.org.

Easy to Read. Hard to Put Down.